To the Peak

Owlkids Books

Chirp, Tweet, and Squawk loved to play in their playhouse. On this particular day, they were playing…

"Mountaineers!" suggested Chirp.

"Climbing Mount Everest!" added Tweet.

"The tallest mountain in the whole wide WORLD!" shouted Squawk.

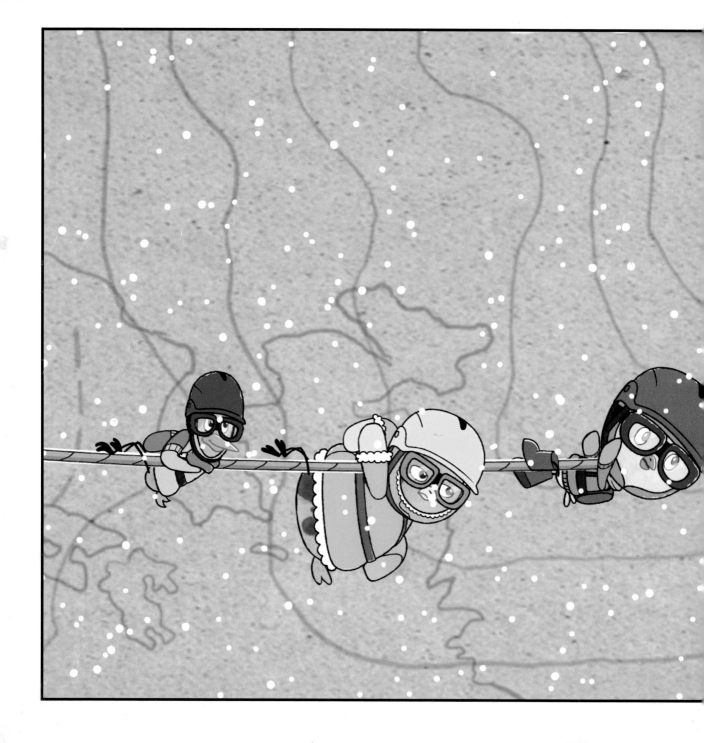

"It takes the strongest of the strong," said Chirp, "the bravest of the brave, the awesomest of the, um…"

"*Awesomest* to make it to the top," said Tweet. "We know, so let's keep going!"

"Actually…" said Squawk, "I just remembered something."

"You can tell us later, Squawk," said Tweet. "We're almost at the peak!"

"But that's just it…I'm afraid of heights," said Squawk.

"What was that?" asked Chirp.

"Our rope broke!" said Tweet.

The strong, brave, and awesome mountaineers found themselves hanging on for dear life to the side of the mountain.

"Oh, no!" said Squawk. "I just remembered something else!"

"Can't you tell us later?" asked Chirp. "Right now, we need to hang on for dear life!"

"I *am* holding on," yelled Squawk. "Because I just remembered that, even more than heights, I'M AFRAID OF FALLING!"

"WHAT WAS THAT?" yelled Squawk.

"Shh!" whispered Tweet. "You'll cause an avalanche!"

"WHAT'S AN AVALANCHE?" yelled Squawk.

"It's when a ton of snow slides down a mountainside," said Tweet.

"THAT'S A THING?" yelled Squawk.

"Yes!" said Chirp. "A thing all of your yelling is causing!"

The mountain *RRRUMBLED* again. Tweet quickly climbed the rope to a ledge. Chirp followed. Squawk did not.

"Pull him up!" said Chirp.

"I *am* pulling!" said Tweet.

"Pull faster!" said Squawk. "Did I mention my fear of heights and even *bigger* fear of falling from them?"

"Phew—thanks, guys! We made it!" said Squawk.

"Actually," said Chirp, "the top of Mount Everest is still over there."

"But with our rope broken, there's no way to get across," said Tweet.

"Wait!" said Chirp. "I might have something in my climber's kit that can help us."

"Climber's kit?" asked Tweet.

"You know," said Chirp, "the climber's kit with all the helpful stuff in it."

"Oh, right!" said Tweet. "That box—I mean, climber's kit…"

"It's in the playhouse! By the front door!" said Squawk. "Let's go get it!"

The three friends opened the lid and looked inside.

"Popsicle sticks, a rubber band, more popsicle sticks, and some glue," said Chirp.

"Lots of popsicle sticks!" said Squawk. "Too bad they're just short pieces of wood."

"Well, one is too short on its own," said Tweet. "But if we put them *together*, we can build a bridge to get across!"

"Great idea, Tweet!" said Chirp.

"To the top!" said Tweet.

"If we must..." said Squawk.

The strong, brave, and awesome mountaineers continued their journey up Mount Everest.

As Chirp and Tweet built a bridge using the popsicle sticks, Squawk made an important discovery...

"Hey, this popsicle stick smells like orange!" yelled Squawk. "I wonder if it also tastes like...YES! IT DOES TASTE LIKE ORANGE!"

SLURRRP!

The mountain began to *RRRUMBLE* again.

"Shh!" said Chirp. "Stop yelling or you'll cause another avalanche!"

"Too late," said Tweet, pointing to the snow rushing down the mountainside.

"BUILD FASTER!" yelled Squawk. "I mean...build faster," he whispered.

"Here comes the avalanche!" cried Chirp as he shoved the leftover popsicle sticks into his backpack. "There's no time to finish the bridge!"

Chirp jumped the rest of the way. Tweet jumped the rest of the way. Squawk did not jump the rest of the way.

"Come on, Squawk!" said Chirp.

"You can do it!" said Tweet.

"Did I mention my fear of heights and even *worse* fear of falling from them?" asked Squawk. "I just remembered *another* thing...

"I'M EVEN MORE AFRAID OF AVALANCHES!" yelled Squawk as he jumped the rest of the way.

The strong, brave, and awesome mountaineers escaped the avalanche. Soon, they were at the peak of Mount Everest.

"We did it!" said Chirp.

"We climbed all the way to the top!" said Tweet.

"WE! ARE! SO! AWESOME!" yelled Squawk.

"Wait! What was that?" asked Chirp.

The mountain began to *RRRUMBLE* once more.

"Your yelling caused *another* avalanche!" said Tweet.

"We have to get off this mountain fast!" said Chirp.

"We still have some popsicle sticks," whispered Squawk. "Let's build…an elevator…or maybe a giant slide…"

"I know!" said Tweet. "A sled!"

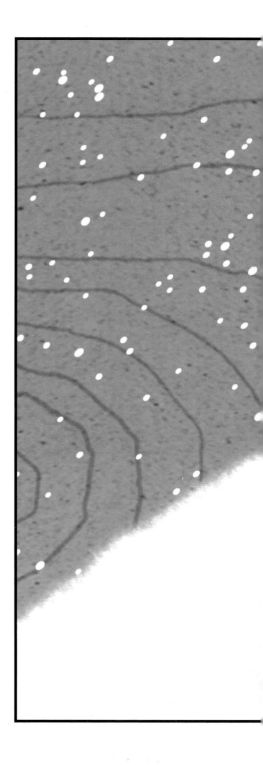

Chirp, Tweet, and Squawk slid all the way down Mount Everest and back into their playhouse.

"And that's the end of another famous mission!" said Chirp.

"Our *coolest* mission yet," said Tweet.

"Is it snack time?" asked Squawk. "I could go for a popsicle right now!"

From an episode of the animated TV series *Chirp*, produced by Sinking Ship (Chirp) Productions. Based on the Chirp character created by Bob Kain.

Based on the TV episode *To the Peak* written by J.J. Johnson.
Story adaptation written by J. Torres.

Owlkids Books acknowledges the financial support of the Canada Council for the Arts, the Ontario Arts Council, the Government of Canada through the Canada Book Fund (CBF) and the Government of Ontario through the Ontario Media Development Corporation's Book Initiative for our publishing activities.

Published in Canada by
Owlkids Books Inc.
10 Lower Spadina Avenue
Toronto, ON M5V 2Z2

Library and Archives Canada Cataloguing in Publication

Torres, J., 1969-, author
        To the peak / adapted by J. Torres.

(Chirp ; 2) Based on the TV program Chirp; writer of the episode: J. J. Johnson.

ISBN 978-1-77147-167-1 (bound).--ISBN 978-1-77147-133-6 (pbk.)

        I. Johnson, J. J., 1980- II. Title. III. Title: Chirp (Television program)

PS8589.O6755667T6 2015   jC813'.54   C2014-908369-6

Edited by: Jessica Burgess
Designed by: Alisa Baldwin

Manufactured in Altona, MB, Canada, in March 2015, by Friesens Corporation
Job #210881

A   B   C   D   E   F

Publisher of Chirp, chickaDEE and OWL
www.owlkidsbooks.com